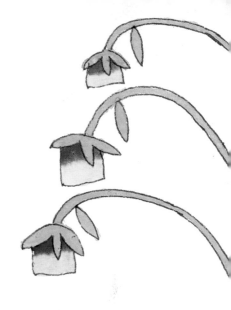

A Beautiful Girl

Amy Schwartz

A NEAL PORTER BOOK
ROARING BROOK PRESS
NEW MILFORD, CONNECTICUT

For Leonard

Copyright © 2006 by Amy Schwartz

A Neal Porter Book

Published by Roaring Brook Press

Roaring Brook Press is a division of Holtzbrinck Publishing Holdings Limited Partnership

143 West Street, New Milford, Connecticut 06776

Distributed in Canada by H. B. Fenn and Company, Ltd.

Library of Congress Cataloging-in-Publication Data

Schwartz, Amy.

A beautiful girl / Amy Schwartz.— 1st ed.

p. cm.

"A Neal Porter book."

Summary: On her way to the market, Jenna encounters an elephant, a robin, a fly, and a goldfish

who discover some of the things that make little girls different from each of them.

ISBN-13: 978-1-59643-165-2   ISBN-10: 1-59643-165-2

[1. Anatomy—Fiction. 2. Animals—Fiction.] I. Title.

PZ7.S406Bea 2006   [E]—dc22   2005033022

JFIC 13

Roaring Brook Press books are available for special promotions and premiums.

For details, contact: Director of Special Markets, Holtzbrinck Publishers.

Printed in China

First edition August 2006

10 9 8 7 6 5 4 3 2 1

On her way to market,

Jenna met
Baby Elephant.
He looked Jenna
up and down.

"You're a funny elephant," he trumpeted. "And you have a very funny trunk."

"Excuse me," Jenna said. "I am not an elephant. I am a big girl and this is my NOSE."

Do you spray water on your
back on a hot, hot day?

"Oh," said Baby Elephant. "Do you
pick up peanuts with your nose?

Do you grab your mother's tail with your nose and follow her through the tall, tall grass?"

"Actually," Jenna said,
"with my nose I smell
daisies and roses.

I smell cookies baking.

I smell Mama when we hug."

"Oh," said Baby Elephant. "You're a very nice girl with a very nice nose. Can I come to the market with you?"

"Yes," Jenna said. "Come along."

Robin flew overhead. She looked
Jenna up and down.

"You're a silly robin," she chirped.
"And you have a very silly beak."

"Excuse me," Jenna said. "I am not a robin.
I am a big girl and this is my MOUTH."

Do you clean your feathers

"Oh," said Robin. "Do you peck
at berries with your mouth?

and build nests with your mouth
and feed your babies worms?"

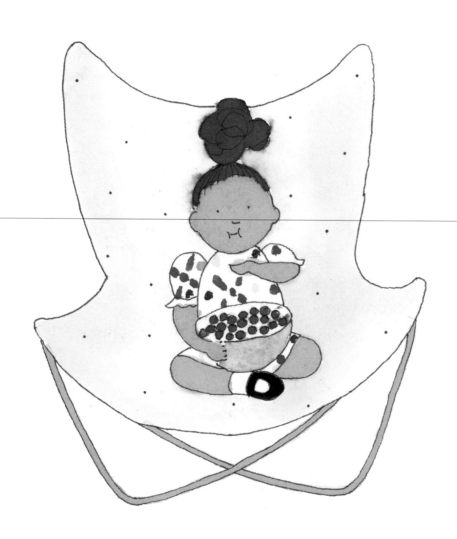

I tell Mama, 'I won't,'

and I tell Baby, 'You'd better! . . .'

"Actually," Jenna said, "with my mouth,
I eat cherries and spit out the pits.

and I give Daddy kisses too."

"Oh," Robin said. "You're a lovely girl with a lovely mouth. Can I come to the market with you?"

"Yes," Jenna said. "Come along."

Fly buzzed by. He looked Jenna
up and down.

"You're a strange fly," he buzzed.
"Where are your 100 eyes?"

"Excuse me," Jenna said.
"I am not a fly.
I am a big girl and
I have TWO EYES."

"Oh," said Fly. "Do you use your two eyes to look for gnats to eat and holes in the window-screen to fly through and big flyswatters to fly away from?"

and at my pretty checked dress

"Actually," Jenna said, "I use my two eyes to look out the window

"Oh," Fly said, "I like you and I like your two eyes too. Can I come to the market with you?"

"Yes," Jenna said, "Come along."

and at my dog, Spot,
and at the clouds in the sky."

Goldfish swam along.
He looked Jenna up and down.

"You're a goofy goldfish," he gurgled.
"And you have very goofy gills."

"Excuse me," Jenna said. "I am not a goldfish,
I am a big girl and these are my EARS."

"Oh," Goldfish said. "Do you use your ears to breathe in and out, in and out, in and out, as you swim up and down the stream?"

"Actually," Jenna said, "I use my ears to listen to Mama singing and Baby crying and Daddy whispering 'I love you.'"

"Oh," Goldfish said. "You're a beautiful girl
with beautiful ears. Can I come
to the market with you?"

"Yes," Jenna said. "Come along."

"Excuse me," Jenna said
at the market. "I would
like some hay, a worm,
a sugar cube, and fish flakes,
please. And a chocolate
cupcake, too."

And they all played together until
Jenna's mama came to fetch her.

"Good-bye," said Baby Elephant. "I'm glad I have a friend with such a nice nose."

"And a lovely mouth," said Robin.

"And two eyes," said Fly.

"And two beautiful ears," said Goldfish. "On such a beautiful girl."

"Who soon will be in her bed and fast asleep," Mama said.

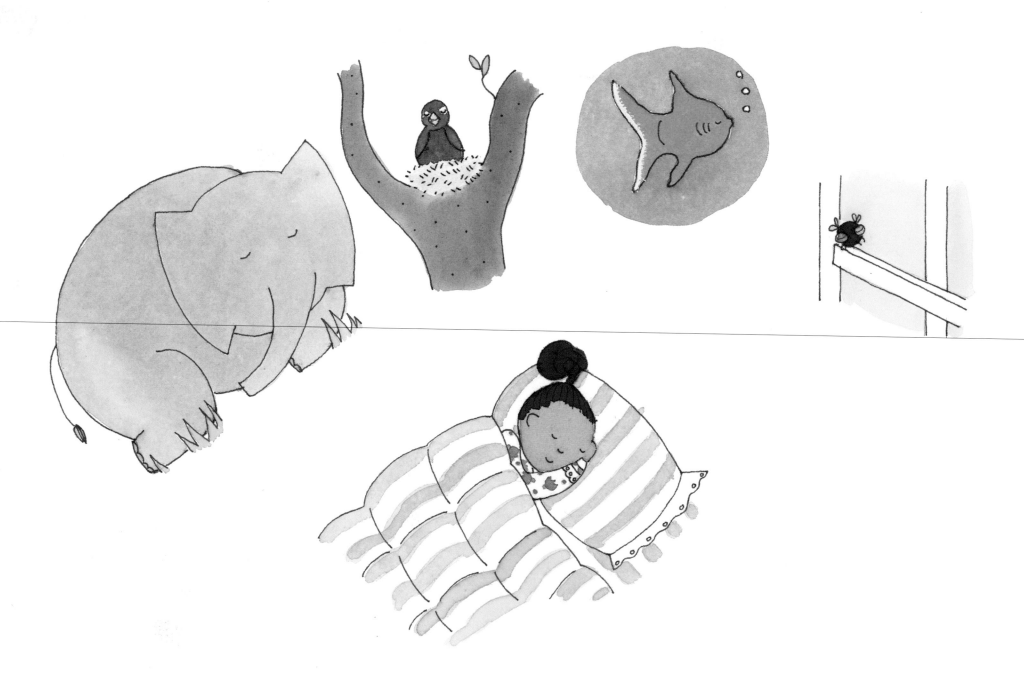

"Just like you."